Captain Cat
and
the Carol Singers

by
Jeremy Lloyd

Illustrated by Graham Percy

Carol arrangements by Daniel Scott

Original music for
'Ring! Ring! We are the Carol Singers'
by Howard Blake

faber and faber
LONDON · BOSTON

Also by Jeremy Lloyd
with illustrations by Graham Percy

The Woodland Gospels
according to Captain Beaky and his Band

The Carols

From the belfry of his church,
Mr Mole, the vicar,
Looked at the falling snow and said,
'My word, it's getting thicker!

'I'll tug the bell rope once or twice
And get them all a-ringing,
Just to let the church mice know
It's time for carol singing.'

Having got the bells to ring,
He dusted off the pews,
Polished up the organ,
And had a little snooze.

Then from the door he heard a knock,
And then he heard a bang –
Then someone kicked it very hard,
And then the doorbell rang.

And so against the icy wind
He pushed the big church door,
And just before his glasses froze
This is what he saw . . .

. . . A cat whose age was clearly great,
With eyes of china blue,
Held out a rather chilly paw
And said, 'How do you do?

'Night was falling, I was cold,
I had no place to stay.
Then through the trees I saw your light
And headed on this way.'

'My tail is frozen to the bone,
I swear it's solid ice.
A nice warm fire would thaw me out,
But a candle would suffice.'

'Come in, come in,' said Vicar Mole,
'Come in and shut the door;
I've never known a Christmas night
As cold as this before.'

'Is it Christmas?' said the cat,
'My word, that's news to me.
By the way, I'm Captain Cat;
I've spent my life at sea.

'My job was catching mice, of course,
That roamed around the ship,
Until old age just slowed me down
And they'd give me the slip.

'So I was cast ashore this time;
They sailed with the tide.
I waved them off till out of sight
And then sat down and cried.

'And then I tramped the countryside
In an endless search
For sanctuary, and by the way,
May I come in the Church?'

Said Vicar Mole, 'You have been bad,
For mice are all my friends.
Eating them's against the rules –
You'll have to make amends.'

'No more mice,' said Captain Cat,
'I promise I won't fail.
But please, dear Vicar, kindly get
A candle for my tail.'

And so two candles later,
And puddles on the floor,
Captain Cat sighed with delight
And felt his tail thaw.

Staring hard at Vicar Mole
With eyes of china blue,
He said, 'Since you've been kind to me,
Then I'll be kind to you.

'I thought you'd make a tasty snack
But haven't got the heart.
And so I'll leave you here in peace,
And silently depart.'

'You have reformed!' cried Vicar Mole,
'I'm glad you've seen the light.
But now I must attend my flock –
Tonight is practice night.

'The carol singers all rehearse,
And, before they leave,
I have to choose the best of them
To sing on Christmas Eve.

'I play the organ and conduct,
And give them all advice.
No sound can make the soul rejoice
Like that of forty mice.'

Said Captain Cat, 'Did I hear right –
That forty was the figure?'
And his eyes of china blue
Got noticeably bigger.

'Dear me, yes,' said Vicar Mole,
And nearly bit his tongue:
'Some of them are frightfully old
And some are very young.

'And none of them is very fat,
For winter food is short.'
'I've noticed that,' said Captain Cat,
'And I've just had a thought.

'Why don't I stay and give a hand,
Like hanging up their coats,
And take the ones that sing off-key
Aside and give them notes?'

'If you insist,' said Vicar Mole,
'But promise to be good.'
'I will indeed,' said Captain Cat,
'Because I said I would.'

Then upon the wooden door
They heard some tiny knocking.
And then a voice cried, 'Open up!
The weather out here's shocking!'

So Captain Cat helped Vicar Mole
To open up the door,
And, as the mice all scampered in,
He counted forty-four!

Harvest mice and church mice
And mice from local houses –
The men all dressed in Sunday best
With hats and gloves and trousers.

The lady mice were smart as well,
In bonnets made of flowers
And homemade little dresses,
That must have taken hours.

Some were very old and bent,
Some short, tall, thin or fat,
And as the door shut with a bang,
A small one shouted, 'Cat!'

They scampered wildly round the church,
And some knelt down to pray,
Till Mole the Vicar raised his hands
And said, 'Don't run away –

'For Captain Cat is quite reformed,
And kindly helping me.'
Said Captain Cat, 'The little ones
Can sit upon my knee.'

There were gasps of 'Oh my word!'
And 'Crumbs!' and 'Well I never!'
And 'Shall we stay?' or 'Shall we go?'
And 'What about the weather?'

As they looked at Captain Cat,
Uncertain what to do,
He fixed them with his bright blue eyes
Of smiling china blue.

He said, 'Dear friends, be not afraid,
For I am old and frail.
I'll help you with your carols
By conducting with my tail.

'There's not a carol I don't know,
For, in a stormy sea,
The sailors sang them all the time
And taught them all to me.'

'I'm glad to hear,' said Vicar Mole,
'That you're so well-informed,
For the carol *Silent Night*
Is now to be performed.'

'Ah, *Silent Night*,' said Captain Cat,
'Well, when still but a kitten,
I heard the strangest story told
Of how that tune was written.

'Apparently some mice, it seems,
Found shelter from the cold
In an organ, in a church –
Well, that's what I was told.

'And as it was in winter time,
And being hungry fellows,
They nibbled at the organ
And made holes in the bellows.

'Then a man sat down to play,
And pressed a note or two,
But to his surprise he heard
A tune completely new.

'So if the mice had not been there
And had a little bite,
He wouldn't have composed a song
Which he called *Silent Night*.'

'That's very true,' said Vicar Mole,
'And it clearly shows us,
That God works in mysterious ways
When mice become composers.'

And seated at the organ
And pointing with his nose,
Said, '*Silent Night*, by Mice and Men.'
And this is how it goes.

Silent Night

Words by Joseph Mohr

Tune by Franz Xavier Gruber

1. Si - lent night! Ho - ly night! All is calm, all is bright

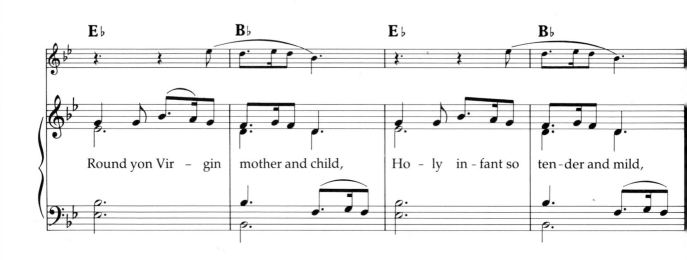

Round yon Vir - gin mother and child, Ho - ly in - fant so ten - der and mild,

Sleep in hea - venly peace, _____ Sleep in hea - venly peace.

2   Silent night! Holy night!
      Shepherds quake at the sight;
      Glories stream from heaven afar,
      Heavenly hosts sing Alleluia;
      Christ, the Saviour, is born,
      Christ, the Saviour, is born.

3   Silent night! Holy night!
      Son of God, love's pure light
      Radiant beams from thy holy face,
      With the dawn of redeeming grace,
      Jesus, Lord, at thy birth,
      Jesus, Lord, at thy birth.

'That was very good,' said Mole,
'So hard to tell who's best.
You all sang very well indeed.
I'm really most impressed.'

'I agree,' said Captain Cat,
'Their voices sounded fine.'
'Oh dear, oh dear,' said Vicar Mole,
'There's only thirty-nine!'

'I'll count again, in case I'm wrong –
Don't tell me you've been naughty!
Oh dear, it's still just thirty-nine
And there were over forty!'

'Don't look at me,' said Captain Cat,
'I haven't laid a finger
On any one of our dear friends,
Each one a splendid singer.

'I must say that the country mice
Have tones extremely clear.
Perhaps that little fat one there
Could stand more over here.'

'Do you mean me?' the fat one squeaked,
'Do that mean I'll be chose?'
'You may well be,' said Captain Cat,
'If you stand very close.

'These ears of mine have perfect pitch;
I've never known them fail.
And as it's getting colder,
I'll warm you with my tail.'

'That's very kind, sir,' said the mouse,
'For being fat, you see,
The other lads do laugh a lot
And they makes fun of me.'

'Most unfair,' said Captain Cat,
And, as he licked his coat,
Said, 'I have every confidence
You'll hit the highest note.'

'Can we get on?' said Vicar Mole,
'We're singing *Three Kings* next.
If these delays continue,
I could get rather vexed.'

Said Captain Cat, 'Forgive me,
For taking so much time.
Three Kings is a carol
That's a favourite of mine.

'It tells how Baby Jesus
In the manger lay
On Christmas morning, which of course,
Was the world's first Christmas Day,

'When three kings from the east appeared,
Which means they travelled far,
Their names were Caspar, Melchior,
And one called Balthazar.

'They came, they said, from Persia,
Where cats have splendid fur,
And with them they brought gifts of gold,
And frankincense and myrrh.

'These, of course, were perfumes
To put upon his brow;
The golden crown meant he was King
Of everybody now.'

Said Vicar Mole, 'How well explained!'
And pointing with his nose
Said, 'Let us sing the *Three Kings* now.'
And this is how it goes.

We Three Kings

Words and tune by J.H. Hopkins

Melchior:

2 Born a king on Bethlehem plain,
  Gold I bring, to crown him again,
  King forever, ceasing never,
  Over us all to reign:
  O, star of wonder, etc.

Caspar:

3 Frankincense to offer have I,
  Incense owns a deity nigh;
  Prayer and praising, all men raising,
  Worship him, God most high:
  O, star of wonder, etc.

Balthazar:

4 Myrrh is mine; its bitter perfume
  Breathes a life of gathering gloom;
  Sorrowing, sighing, bleeding, dying,
  Sealed in a stone-cold tomb:
  O, star of wonder, etc.

All:

5 Glorious now behold him arise,
  King and God and sacrifice.
  Heav'n sings alleluia,
  Alleluia the earth replies:
  O, star of wonder, etc.

'What joy, what bliss!' said Vicar Mole,
'So hard to tell who's best.
You all sang frightfully well indeed.
I'm really most impressed.'

'I agree,' said Captain Cat.
'They sounded good to me.'
'Oh dear, oh dear,' said Vicar Mole,
'There's only thirty-three!

'I'll count again, in case I'm wrong;
Don't tell me you've been naughty.
Oh, no – it's only thirty-three,
And there were over forty!'

Said Captain Cat, 'That's very strange –
I didn't see them leave.
Could one be in my pocket,
Or hiding up my sleeve?

'No, there's nothing there but me;
I'm sure they'll show up soon.
Perhaps they're in the vestry,
Rehearsing a new tune.'

They searched the vestry and the church,
In every nook and cranny,
While relatives called out their names
Like 'Tiny Tim, Aunt Annie!

'The Cheesey Boys and Nibbler Ned,
Old Grandma Mouse and James,
And Nosey Norman, show yourselves,
And please stop playing games.'

A bearded mouse with walking stick
Waved it around his head.
'It's that cat – I'm sure of it.
We're going to end up dead!

'I swear he's fatter than he was,
For cats are all born mousers.
If he lays one paw on me,
I'll jump out of my trousers!'

'I promise you,' said Captain Cat,
'With hand upon my heart,
Just like you, I never saw
A single mouse depart.

'May lightning strike my tail at once
If I've not told the truth.'
All the mice looked up expecting
Lightning through the roof.

To their surprise no thunder rolled,
No sudden flash of light.
'It just could be,' said Vicar Mole,
'That Captain Cat is right.

'He didn't notice where they went,
And, strangely, nor did I.'
'I'm glad of that,' said Captain Cat,
'I could not tell a lie.'

A lady mouse, in floral dress
And bonnet made of straw,
Said, 'Where's my little fat boy gone?
I can't see him no more!'

'He was just here,' said Captain Cat,
'I had my tail around him.
Ah, here he is, beneath this pew;
Thank heaven that we've found him!

'Tell me, boy, what is your name?'
The mouse said, 'Little Fred.
And it's not easy singing
With your tail round my head.

'Your whiskers have got up my nose,
My tonsils are all tickly.
I'll have to have a good cough now.'
Said Vicar Mole, 'Well, quickly.

'We must get on; it's getting late,
And I have made the choice:
We're singing *Good King Wenceslas* –
A good test for your voice.'

'A lovely carol,' said the cat,
'About the Feast of Stephen,
When, like tonight, the snow was thick,
And deep and crisp and even.

'But do you know who Stephen was?
Now, each one, rack your brain.'
'Didn't he invent,' said Fred,
'The very first steam train?'

Vicar Mole mopped at his brow
With a hanky from his pocket.
'That was Stephenson,' he said,
'The train was called the Rocket.

'Now, if you'd paid attention,
And you'd read your Bibles,
You'd know that Stephen was a friend
Of Jesus's disciples.

'Now please don't let me down again,
And all of you remember,
He lost his life to become a saint
On the 26th December.

'Saints, of course, are people,
Who've been especially good.
All I'll be remembered for
Is homemade Christmas pud.'

Then Vicar Mole sat down to play,
And pointing with his nose,
Said 'Let's sing *Good King Wenceslas*.'
And this is how it goes.

Good King Wenceslas

Words by J.M. Neale

2 'Hither, page, and stand by me,
    If thou know'st it, telling,
  Yonder peasant, who is he?
    Where and what his dwelling?'
  'Sire, he lives a good league hence,
    Underneath the mountain,
  Right against the forest fence,
    By Saint Agnes' fountain.'

3 'Bring me flesh and bring me wine,
    Bring me pine-logs hither:
  Thou and I will see him dine,
    When we bear them thither.'
  Page and monarch, forth they went,
    Forth they went together;
  Through the rude wind's wild lament
    And the bitter weather.

4 'Sire, the night is darker now,
    And the wind blows stronger;
  Fails my heart, I know not how;
    I can go no longer.'
  'Mark my footsteps, good my page;
    Tread thou in them boldly:
  Thou shalt find the winter's rage
    Freeze thy blood less coldly.'

5 In his master's steps he trod,
    Where the snow lay dinted;
  Heat was in the very sod
    Which the Saint had printed.
  Therefore, Christian men, be sure,
    Wealth or rank possessing,
  Ye who now will bless the poor,
    Shall yourself find blessing.

'Harmonious!' said Vicar Mole.
'So hard to tell who's best.
You all sang frightfully well indeed –
I'm really quite impressed.'

'I agree,' said Captain Cat,
'Those voices were pure heaven.'
'Oh dear, oh dear,' said Vicar Mole,
'There's only twenty-seven!

'I'll count again, in case I'm wrong;
Don't tell me you've been naughty.
Oh no, it's only twenty-seven
And there were over forty!'

Said Captain Cat, 'That's very odd
That they should disappear.
After all, it's cold outside,
And nice and warm in here.

'Perhaps we ought to stop awhile
And pause to have some tea.
But why is it those little mice
All stare so hard at me?'

'They think, perhaps,' said Vicar Mole,
'That as they're getting less,
It could be that you've eaten them.
Of course, it's just a guess.'

'I'm most disturbed,' said Captain Cat,
'By even the suggestion.
The very thought has given me
Quite awful indigestion.

'Perhaps you'd care to take my hand,
Together we shall search
To see if they are hiding
In the belfry of the Church.'

Said Vicar Mole, 'It's dark up there –
My eyes are very weak.'
Said Captain Cat, 'But mine are not,
So let's go forth and seek.'

So up the creaky stairs they went:
The old Mole held the candle,
And at the belfry door he stopped
And turned the wooden handle.

'You go first,' said Vicar Mole.
The door creaked open wide.
Captain Cat went in – and bang!
The door shut him inside.

'I'm sorry, Cat,' said Vicar Mole,
'And now I must retire
Back down the stairs to practise
With what's left of my choir.'

'Let me out!' cried Captain Cat.
'It wasn't me, I swear!'
But his only answer was
The footsteps on the stair.

'He thinks,' said Captain Cat, 'I'm trapped,
But while there's life, there's hope.
And there's not a ship's cat born
Who can't climb down a rope.'

Down in the church, old Vicar Mole
Said, 'Let's continue singing.'
Then to his dismay he heard
The big old church bell ringing . . .

It dinged and donged, and donged and dinged,
And then across a rafter
They saw the shadow of a cat
And heard a peal of laughter.

And down a curtain, near the front,
Climbed old Captain Cat,
And said, 'Those missing mice weren't there –
You can be sure of that.'

And gazing round, with great big eyes
Of smiling china blue,
Said, 'Now I'm ready to go on.
And so, I hope, are you.'

'Forgive me, please,' said Vicar Mole.
Said Captain Cat, 'What for?
For surely it was just the wind
That blew and shut the door.'

'How glad I am,' said Vicar Mole,
'That that is what you think.'
And blushing right down to his tail,
He turned completely pink,

And sitting at the organ,
And pointing with his nose,
Said, '*Holly and the Ivy*, next.
And this is how it goes.'

'Not so fast,' said Captain Cat,
'I'd like to take this chance
To tell you all about that song –
The music comes from France.'

'*Bon* news indeed!' said Vicar Mole,
'And *la grande surprise*!
Would you like to tell us more,
Or may I start now, please?'

Said Captain Cat, 'Before we do
I have some information;
The holly is not only there
For Christmas decoration.

'When the holly bears the berry,
It means a child is born,
Just as Jesus Christ was
On that Christmas morn.'

Said one church mouse, 'Well, I am blessed!
I never knew all that.
Fancy all that knowledge,
Coming from a cat.'

Said Vicar Mole, 'If we can start,
I'm ready with the key.
I'll pick the ones who sing the best,
And then we'll have some tea.'

And pumping up the organ,
And pointing with his nose,
Called '*Holly and the Ivy*, choir.'
And this is how it goes.

4

The Holly and the Ivy

English traditional carol

1. The hol-ly and the i - vy, When they are both full - grown, Of all the trees that are in the wood, The holly bears the crown. The ris - ing of the sun And the run - ning of the deer, The play - ing of the mer - ry or - gan, Sweet sing - ing in the choir.

2   The holly bears a blossom,
    As white as the lily flower,
    And Mary bore sweet Jesus Christ,
    To be our sweet Saviour:
    The rising of the sun, etc.

3   The holly bears a berry,
    As red as any blood,
    And Mary bore sweet Jesus Christ
    To do poor sinners good:
    The rising of the sun, etc.

4   The holly bears a prickle,
    As sharp as any thorn,
    And Mary bore sweet Jesus Christ
    On Christmas day in the morn:
    The rising of the sun, etc.

5   The holly bears a bark,
    As bitter as any gall,
    And Mary bore sweet Jesus Christ
    For to redeem us all:
    The rising of the sun, etc.

6   The holly and the ivy,
    When they are both full grown,
    Of all the trees that are in the wood,
    The holly bears the crown.
    The rising of the sun, etc.

'Bravo, bravo,' said Vicar Mole,
'So hard to say who's best.
You all sang frightfully well indeed.
I'm really most impressed.'

'I agree,' said Captain Cat,
'They were the best they've been.'
'Oh dear, oh dear,' said Vicar Mole,
'There's only seventeen!

'I'll count again, in case I'm wrong;
Don't tell me you've been naughty.
Oh no – it's only seventeen,
And there were over forty!'

Said Captain Cat, 'I am amazed:
I didn't see a thing.
But, of course, my eyes were closed –
They do that when I sing.

'Mind you, have you noticed
That the best ones are still here?
Only those with weaker voices
Seem to disappear.

'The tea you spoke of recently
Has not appeared as yet.
I thought I'd better mention it,
In case you should forget.'

'I'm glad you did,' said Vicar Mole,
'Now pay attention, choir.
We'll take tea in the vestry
And I will light the fire.'

And over tea old Captain Cat
Told with some elation
Of his exciting times at sea,
But not his occupation!

As he spoke old Vicar Mole,
Closed his eyes and prayed
For forgiveness and salvation,
For a cat who'd strayed.

And then with no one looking
He knelt upon his knees,
And said, 'Dear Lord, please fill this cat
With biscuits, tea and cheese.

'Make sure there's not the slightest room
For any mouse to be.
But most of all, Dear Lord, I pray,
Please don't leave room for me.'

'Wake up, Mole,' said Captain Cat,
'We cannot have you failing.
What's the next song going to be?'
Said Mole, *Three Ships a-Sailing.*

'And if you sat down next to me,
Providing that there's room,
You could pump the bellows up,
While I pick out the tune.'

So back they went, and Captain Cat
Sat on the organ seat,
And blew the bellows up to full,
By pumping with his feet.

'Steady on,' said Vicar Mole,
'Listen to that squeaking.
You've blown the bellows up too far –
I fear they've started leaking.

'The organ's old, and needs repair;
Your legs are far too strong.
I'd better do it on my own.
Now, stand by for the song.'

So Vicar Mole sat down to play,
And pointing with his nose
Said, '*I Saw Three Ships a-Sailing*.'
And this is how it goes.

5

I Saw Three Ships Come Sailing In

English traditional carol

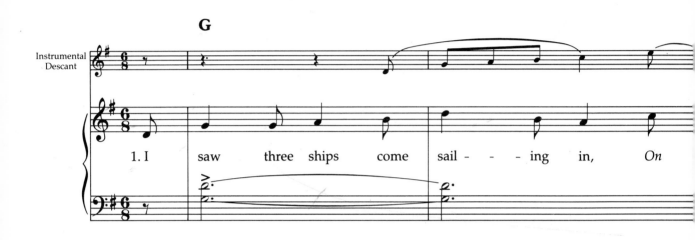

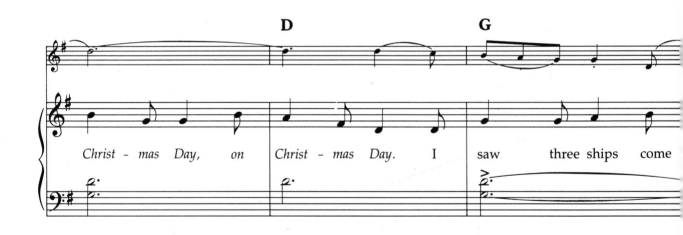

2 And what was in those ships all three?
On Christmas Day, etc.

3 Our Saviour Christ and his lady.
On Christmas Day, etc.

4 Pray, whither sailed those ships all three?
On Christmas Day, etc.

5 O, they sailed into Bethlehem.
On Christmas Day, etc.

6 And all the bells on earth shall ring.
On Christmas Day, etc.

7 And all the angels in heaven shall sing.
On Christmas Day, etc.

8 And all the souls on earth shall sing.
On Christmas Day, etc.

9 Then let us all rejoice amain!
On Christmas Day, etc.

'Perfect pitch,' said Vicar Mole,
'So hard to tell who's best.
You all sang frightfully well indeed;
I'm really most impressed.'

'I agree,' said Captain Cat,
'Some better than myself.'
'Oh dear, oh dear,' said Vicar Mole,
'For now there's only twelve!

'I'll count again, in case I'm wrong;
Don't tell me you've been naughty.
Oh no, it's only twelve this time
And there were over forty!'

Said Captain Cat, 'I'm going mad.
Where have those dear mice gone?
If we continue on like this,
We could be down to one.'

Just then a shadow crossed the wall
And gave a ghostly howl,
And there alighted on a pew
A very large barn owl.

'Good evening all,' the owl intoned,
'I heard your bell a-ringing,
And so I changed my flight plan
And came this way a-winging.

'I flew in through the belfry tower
Not knowing whom I'd meet.
How nice to find so many mice –
It's quite a Christmas treat.'

And then he went to snatch a mouse,
But something made him pause,
As Captain Cat said, 'Don't do that',
And pointed to his claws.

Then he carefully sharpened them
On the cold stone floor
Then polished them beneath his chin
And sharpened them some more.

The owl flapped back on to his perch
And blinked his yellow eyes,
And ruffled all his feathers up
To look a bigger size,

Pretending that he'd never thought
To have a little snack;
But to reassure them all
He hopped a few pews back.

'I think,' said Little Fred, the mouse,
'That we should give a cheer
For Captain Cat, for, without him,
We wouldn't all be here.'

'You're not all here,' his father said,
'Our number is depleted.
So if you can't talk sensible,
Just sit down and be seated.'

Said Captain Cat, 'We'd better start!'
Said Vicar Mole, 'Quite right!
If we don't get a move on
We could be here all night.'

And sitting at the organ,
And pointing with his nose,
Said, 'Angels from the Realms is next.'
And this is how it goes.

6

Angels, from the Realms of Glory

Words by
James Montgomery

Old French tune

2   Shepherds in the fields abiding,
Watching o'er your flocks by night,
God with man is now residing,
Yonder shines the infant light:
Gloria in excelsis Deo.

3   Sages, leave your contemplations;
Brighter visions beam afar;
Seek the great desire of nations;
Ye have seen his natal star:
Gloria in excelsis Deo.

4   Saints before the altar bending,
Watching long in hope and fear,
Suddenly the Lord, descending,
In his temple shall appear:
Gloria in excelsis Deo.

5   Though an infant now we view him,
He shall fill his father's throne,
Gather all the nations to him;
Every knee shall then bow down:
Gloria in excelsis Deo.

'Emotional,' said Vicar Mole,
'So hard to tell who's best.
You all sang frightfully well indeed,
I'm really most impressed.'

'I agree,' said Captain Cat,
'They really sounded great.'
'Oh dear, oh dear,' said Vicar Mole,
'I've only counted eight!

'I'll count again, in case I'm wrong;
Don't tell me you've been naughty.
Oh no – it's only eight again.
And there were over forty!'

'Shiver my timbers,' said the Cat,
'That's what they say at sea.
But I haven't moved from here,
So don't all look at me.'

Said Vicar Mole, 'With only eight,
It is the end – amen.'
Said Captain Cat, 'Without the owl,
There's you and me – that's ten.

'And ten can make a splendid sound
And what's more I forgot,
The fat one's in my pocket still –
That makes it quite a lot.'

And taking out the little mouse,
He tickled 'neath his chin,
And said, 'It must be hot in there –
You've come out rather thin.'

'It was indeed,' said Little Fred,
'Now where's my Mum and Dad?'
Said Vicar Mole, 'They've disappeared:
You must be very sad.'

'I am, of course,' said Little Fred,
'But I've been left behind
To carry on the family name,
So I don't really mind.

'And back at home I've sisters
And brothers by the score,
And by the time I get back there,
I expect there'll be some more.'

The barn owl gazed at Little Fred,
And said, 'I must confess,
I'd be obliged if, when you go,
You'd leave me your address.'

'He won't do that,' said Captain Cat,
'Of that you can be sure,
For I myself will see him home.
Quite safely, to his door.'

'How very kind,' said Vicar Mole,
And patted Little Fred.
'Perhaps you ought to do it now,
It's time he was in bed.'

Vicar Mole went to the doors,
And threw them open wide.
A mighty wind filled up the church
And blew the owl outside.

Through the whirling snow and trees,
He disappeared from view.
The last thing that they heard from him
Was – yes, you've guessed it – 'Whooo . . .'

'Oh, well done,' said Captain Cat,
And putting down his head,
Into the snowy night he went.
'I'll be back soon,' he said.

Vicar Mole slammed shut the doors,
And bolted them up tight,
And said, 'Dear Lord, I thank you:
I knew I'd be all right.

'I'm sure that if that cat had stayed,
That we'd all end up dead.
But horrors! I've just had a thought –
What of poor Little Fred?

'Forgive this weak and selfish mole,
For, to preserve my health,
I've just abandoned a small mouse
And all to save myself!'

And then a window in the church
Squeaked and opened wide,
And Captain Cat said, 'Well, that's that!'
And bounded back inside.

And from his jacket pocket
Out popped a little head,
Which said, 'No one would let me in,
'Cos they was all in bed.'

Said Vicar Mole, 'The Lord be praised,
And no more mice I'm losing.
Now let me see which carol's next –
Ah, here's the one I'm choosing.

'A splendid song for Christmas,
A verse for every day.
We can all sing different parts
Just like a roundelay.'

And sitting at the organ
And pointing with his nose,
Said, *The Twelve Days of Christmas.*'
And this is how it goes.

7

The Twelve Days of Christmas

English traditional carol.

* Sing appropriate number of day, then cut from † to appropriate boxed number.

'Each day was good,' said Vicar Mole,
'It's hard to tell who's best.
What's left of you sing frightfully well,
I'm really most impressed.'

'I agree,' said Captain Cat,
'But just a moment – wait!
I don't think we've lost a mouse,
'Cos I've just counted eight!'

Said Mole, 'Well, I'll just count myself,
In case that you've been naughty.
Oh yes, I've counted eight of them –
But there were over forty.

'Still, I'm relieved,' said Vicar Mole,
'At least we've stopped the rot.
But where the rest went, heaven knows;
I wonder where they've got?

'While we're winning, let's proceed,
And sing another song.
I think I've picked the ones I want,
But then, I could be wrong.

'The trouble is the organ.
The pedal's stiff and strange,
And some notes do not play at all,
Inhibiting my range.'

'Perhaps you need,' said Captain Cat,
'Some nice hot candle grease.
We'll drop it in the working parts,
And see if they release.'

And taking lots of candles,
They set them all alight
And held them so the hot wax dripped
Straight down an organ pipe.

Vicar Mole peered down the pipe,
And when he'd finished peeking,
He pushed the pedals up and down,
And listened to them squeaking.

'How very odd,' said Vicar Mole,
And pushed the pedals quicker.
Said Captain Cat, 'Good gracious me,
They're squeaking louder, Vicar.'

'Never mind,' said Vicar Mole,
'And let us now proceed.
'Oh dear, I'm sitting on a song,
And it's the one I need.

'*God Rest You Merry, Gentlemen*,
A cheerful carol, that.
And *God rest* means God keep you safe.'
'I know that,' said the Cat.

Vicar Mole pressed down the keys
And pointed with his nose:
'*God Rest You Merry, Gentlemen.*'
And this is how it goes.

8

God Rest You Merry, Gentlemen

English traditional carol

1. God rest you merry, gentlemen, Let nothing you dis - may, For Jesus Christ our Sa - viour was born up - on this day, To save us all from Satan's power When we were gone a - stray. O ___ tid - ings of com - fort and joy, comfort and joy, O ___ tid - ings of com - fort and joy.

2 From God our heav'nly Father
A blessed angel came,
And unto certain shepherds
Brought tidings of the same,
How that in Bethlehem was born
The son of God by name:
O tidings of comfort, etc

3 The shepherds at those tidings
Rejoiced much in mind,
And left their flocks a-feeding,
In tempest, storm, and wind,
And went to Bethlehem straight-way
This blessed babe to find:
O tidings of comfort, etc

4 But when to Bethlehem they came,
Whereat this infant lay,
They found him in a manger,
Where oxen feed on hay;
His mother Mary kneeling,
Unto the Lord did pray:
O tidings of comfort, etc

5 Now to the Lord sing praises,
All you within this place,
And with true love and brotherhood
Each other now embrace;
This holy tide of Christmas
All others doth deface:
O tidings of comfort, etc

'That was extra good,' said Mole,
'Not hard to tell who's best.
All of you sang very well;
I'm really most impressed.'

'I agree,' said Captain Cat,
And gave his chin two licks.
'Oh dear, oh dear,' said Vicar Mole;
'I've counted only six!

'I'll count again, in case I'm wrong;
Don't tell me you've been naughty.
No, there's only six of them,
And there were over forty!'

'Two of them,' said Captain Cat,
'Were just here by my side.
Now where could they have got to?
There's nowhere they could hide.'

'I'm still here,' said Little Fred,
Beneath the Vicar's hat.
'I'm most relieved,' said Vicar Mole.
'Me too,' said Captain Cat.

'But at least we have a choir
To sing at Christmas time.
I think that we should celebrate
And have a glass of wine.'

So round the vestry fire they sat
And warmed their hands and feet,
And after a few sips of wine,
They dozed off in the heat.

Vicar Mole, who snored a lot,
Then dreamed that Captain Cat
Had swallowed him, and in the dark,
He couldn't find his hat.

And round him were the missing mice
And, much to his surprise,
They were all accusing him
Of causing their demise.

He lit a candle in his dream,
But all that he could see,
Were lots of mice, all swimming round
In biscuits, cheese and tea.

He woke up with an awful start,
Holding up the candle,
To find the cat had taught the mice
A lullaby by Handel.

As their voices hummed the tune,
Each one a perfect note,
Little Fred gave Mole a wave
From the Captain's coat.

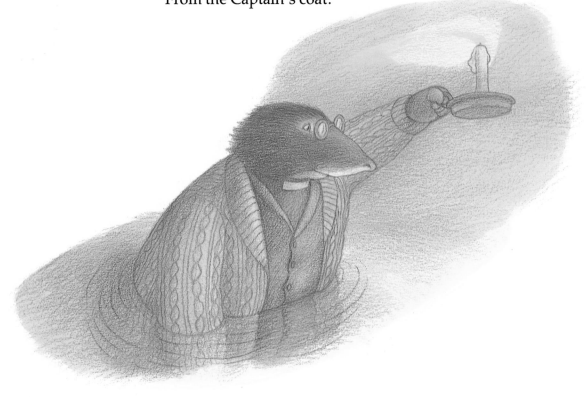

'That's very good,' said Captain Cat,
'Your voices are divine.
Let me give you all a hug.'
Said Vicar Mole, 'No time.

'We've still a carol left unsung,
And then we have to choose
What order we will sing them in
And which ones we will use.

'So follow me back down the aisle,
There's one I want to hear.
The time for it's appropriate,
For midnight is quite near.'

And seated at the organ,
And pointing with his nose,
Said, *It Came Upon the Midnight Clear.*
And this is how it goes.

9

It Came Upon a Midnight Clear

Words by
Edmund H. Sears

Traditional English tune.

2   Still through the cloven skies they come,
    With peaceful wings unfurled;
    And still their heav'nly music floats
    O'er all the weary world;
    Above its sad and lowly plains
    They bend on hov'ring wing;
    And ever o'er its Babel sounds
    The blessed angels sing.

3   Yet with the woes of sin and strife
    The world has suffered long;
    Beneath the angel strain have rolled
    Two thousand years of wrong;
    And man, at war with man, hears not
    The love song which they bring;
    O hush the noise, ye men of strife,
    And hear the angels sing!

4   For lo! The days are hast'ning on,
    By prophet-bards foretold,
    When, with the ever-circling years,
    Comes round the age of gold;
    When peace shall over all the earth
    Its ancient splendours fling,
    And the whole world sends back the song
    Which now the angels sing.

'That wasn't frightfully good,' said Mole,
'It's hard to tell who's best
When not a single note was heard.
I'm really not impressed.'

'I agree,' said Captain Cat,
'Thought I'd gone quite deaf.'
'Oh dear, oh dear,' cried Vicar Mole,
'There are no mices left!

'I'll count again, in case I'm wrong;
Don't tell me you've been naughty.
No, there's not a single one,
And there were over forty.'

And taking off his spectacles,
Vicar Mole looked shocked.
'When Bishop Bunny hears of this,
I know I'll be defrocked!

'Oh where, oh where have they all gone?
I'm sure that you're the culprit.'
Said Captain Cat, 'Look over there –
A mouse upon your pulpit!

'And what is more, it's Little Fred –
Now tell me where you've been.'
'With the rest,' said Little Fred,
'Inside that old machine.

'When you said that mice invented
Silent Night by biting through
Ancient bellows in an organ,
They climbed in and had a chew.

'Now it's got more holes than cheeses,
Forty-four have had a bite,
In the hope the notes created
Sound as good as *Silent Night*.'

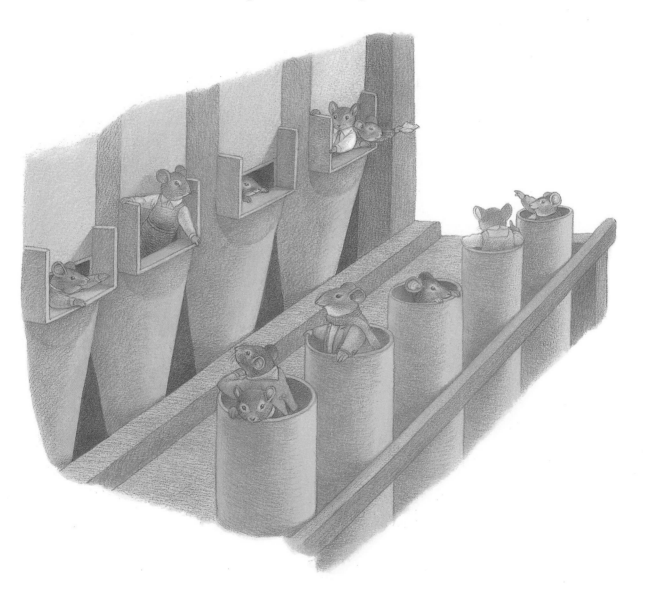

Said the Mole, 'Dear Lord, forgive me,
For I have misjudged the cat!
But I wonder if the organ
Will be working after that.

'Now, come out and we will try it.'
And, as all the rest appeared,
Vicar Mole pressed on the pedals
And exclaimed, 'Just as I feared.

'All the notes are in a jumble,
Flats and sharps are strangely changed,
And the sound of this old organ,
Is completely re-arranged.'

But the tune the organ played now
Was as sweet as any bird's.
So the Vicar got some paper
And the mice composed the words.

Captain Cat, in his best writing,
Helped them get the spelling right.
So they sat up, all composing,
Until it was nearly light.

Then Vicar Mole sat at the organ,
Of course, he pointed with his nose,
And played the 'chewn' that they had bitten,
And this is how their carol goes . . .

10

Ring! Ring! We are the Carol Singers

Words by Jeremy Lloyd

Music by Howard Blake

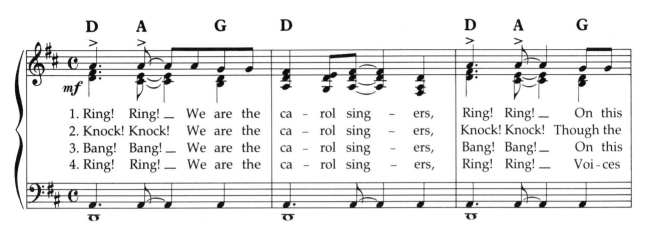

1. Ring! Ring! __ We are the ca - rol sing - ers, Ring! Ring! __ On this
2. Knock! Knock! We are the ca - rol sing - ers, Knock! Knock! Though the
3. Bang! Bang! __ We are the ca - rol sing - ers, Bang! Bang! __ On this
4. Ring! Ring! __ We are the ca - rol sing - ers, Ring! Ring! __ Voi - ces

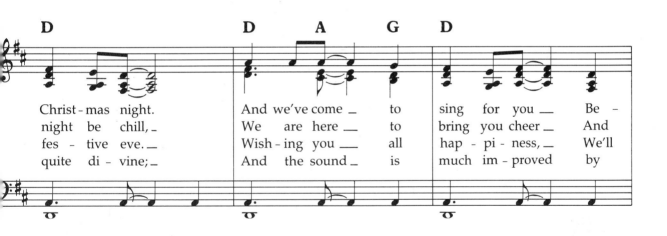

Christ - mas night. And we've come __ to sing for you __ Be -
night be chill, __ We are here __ to bring you cheer __ And
fes - tive eve. __ Wish - ing you __ all hap - pi - ness, __ We'll
quite di - vine; __ And the sound __ is much im - proved by

-cause we saw __ your light. All wrapped up __ in
hope our poc - - kets fill. We'll sing you 'Good King
sing be - fore __ we leave, 'God Rest You Mer - ry,
bis - cuits, cheese __ and wine. But should you bid __ us

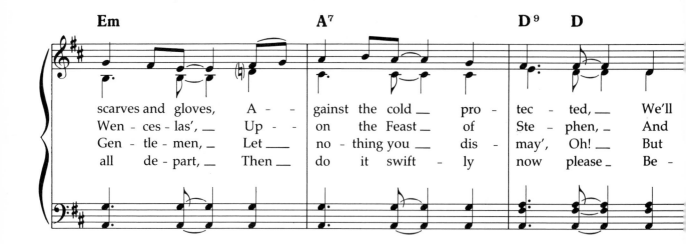

scarves and gloves, A — — gainst the cold __ pro — tec — ted, __ We'll
Wen — ces — las', __ Up — — on the Feast __ of Ste — phen, __ And
Gen — tle — men, __ Let __ no — thing you __ dis — may', Oh! __ But
all de — part, __ Then __ do it swift — ly now please _ Be —

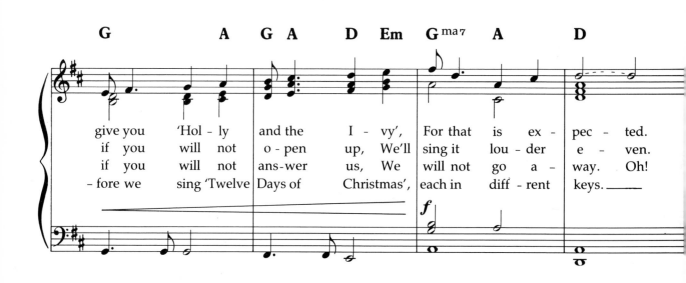

give you 'Hol — ly and the I — vy', For that is ex — pec — ted.
if you will not o — pen up, We'll sing it lou — der e — ven.
if you will not ans — wer us, We will not go a — way. Oh!
— fore we sing 'Twelve Days of Christmas', each in diff — rent keys. ____

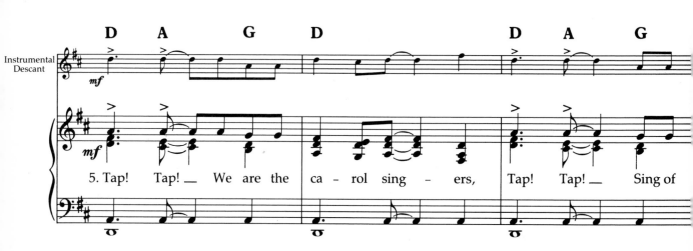

Instrumental
Descant

5. Tap! Tap! __ We are the ca — rol sing — ers, Tap! Tap! __ Sing of

First published in 1986
by Faber and Faber Limited
3 Queen Square London WC1N 3AU

Photoset by Parker Typesetting Service, Leicester
Printed in Great Britain by
W S Cowell Ltd, Ipswich

British Library Cataloguing in Publication Data

Lloyd, Jeremy
Captain Cat and the carol singers.
I. Title   II. Percy, Graham
821'.914   PR6062.L64
ISBN 0-571-14541-8